Watching Whales

Contents

Leading a whale watch 2

Stellwagen Bank 3

A whale-watch expert 4

Where are the whales? 6

Whales of the Atlantic Ocean 8

Do whales have teeth? 10

A curious whale 12

Humpback surprise 14

A whale needs help 16

People and whales 18

Strange creatures 20

Glossary 21

Whale watching diary 22

Are you ready to go and watch whales?

Written and illustrated by Karen Romano Young

Collins

Leading a whale watch

Joanne Jarzobski works on Captain Mark's boat. She helps whale watchers to spot whales and understand what they are seeing.

Joanne has led more than 1,600 whale watches to Stellwagen Bank, 30 miles from the coast of Massachusetts, in the United States of America.

We're going to Stellwagen Bank today.

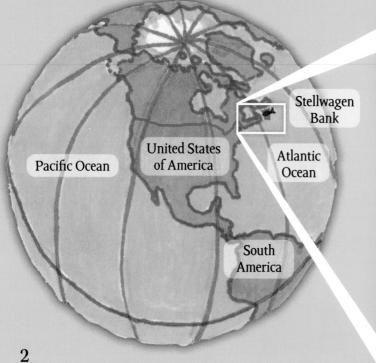

Stellwagen Bank

Pacific Ocean

United States of America

Atlantic Ocean

South America

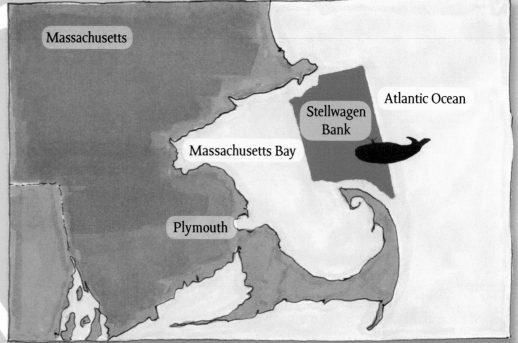

Massachusetts

Atlantic Ocean

Stellwagen Bank

Massachusetts Bay

Plymouth

Stellwagen Bank

At Stellwagen Bank the sea floor drops sharply like an underwater cliff. The ocean water is forced upwards against the cliff, carrying fish and tiny animals called krill to the top. Whales come here to eat them.

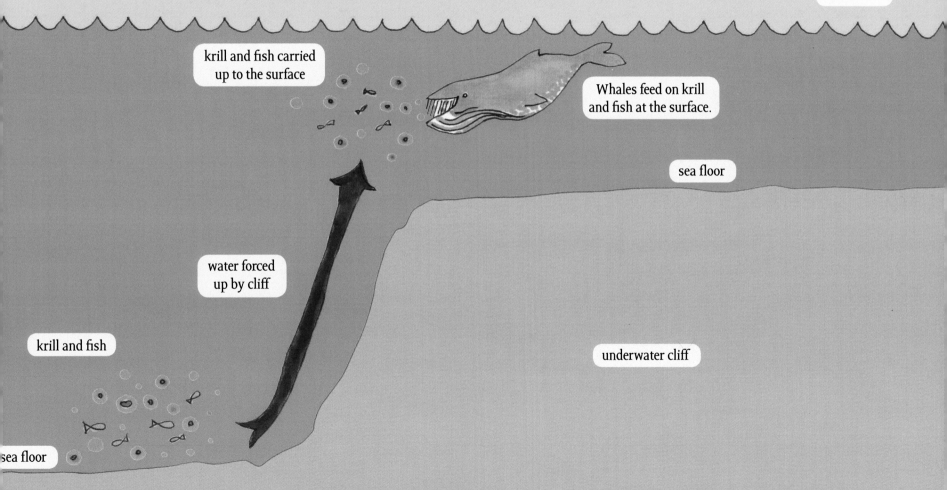

sea surface

krill and fish carried up to the surface

Whales feed on krill and fish at the surface.

sea floor

water forced up by cliff

krill and fish

underwater cliff

sea floor

3

A whale-watch expert

Joanne went on her first whale watch when she was seven years old. She saw her first whale, Salt, along with her **calf**, Crystal. Joanne wanted to learn about the whales and to share what she found out.

People go whale watching to learn more about whales.

Whales can be harmed by ships, **pollution**, noise, fishing gear and lines. Some people hunt whales for food, but many feel that these gentle, intelligent animals should be left alone.

Where are the whales?

Whales swim thousands of miles each year.

In spring they swim north to Stellwagen Bank for the summer. In the autumn, as it gets colder, they go south to warmer waters to **breed**.

These warm waters are safe for calves, but there isn't much food there. By the time the whales return to Stellwagen in the next spring, they're hungry.

To see our first whale, you've got to watch the water, folks.

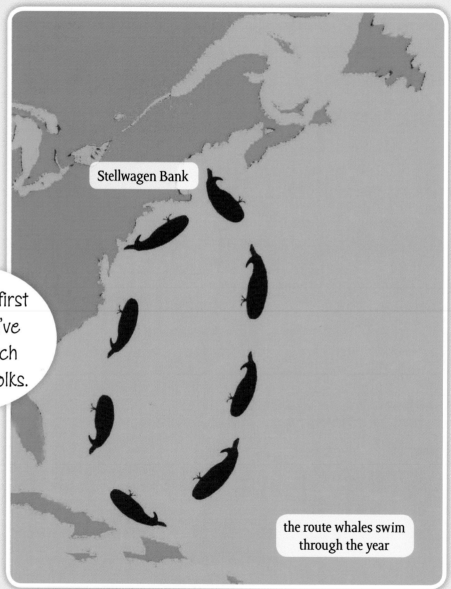

Stellwagen Bank

the route whales swim through the year

6

Whales of the Atlantic Ocean

Here are some of the whales that have been spotted in the Atlantic Ocean.

pilot whales

white-sided dolphin

orca (killer whales)

humpback whale and calf

sperm whale

Whales breathe air through a **blowhole** on the top of their head. It's possible to identify a whale by its **blow**.

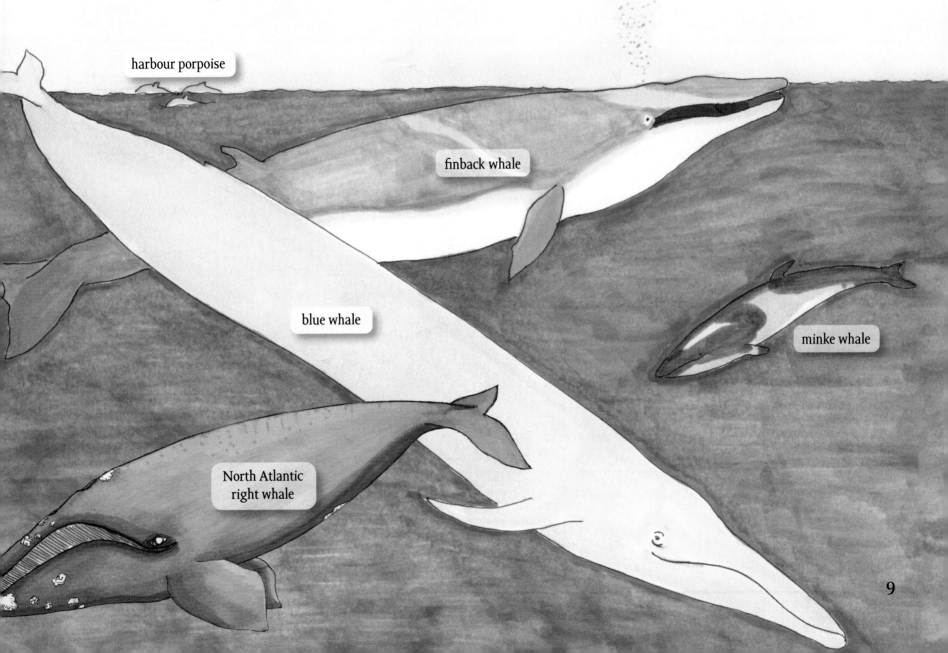

harbour porpoise

finback whale

blue whale

minke whale

North Atlantic
right whale

9

Do whales have teeth?

Orca, sperm whales, pilot whales and dolphins have teeth but blue whales, humpbacks, finbacks and right whales have **baleen** hanging from the roof of their mouth. When the whale takes a gulp of water, the baleen **filters** any food and traps it in the whale's mouth.

Whales' teeth are big and sharp.

Baleen is strong and bendy, a bit like human fingernails.

blowhole

baleen

tail flukes

Whales that have baleen eat two to four tonnes of food a day. That's a lot of gulps of water!

North Atlantic right whale

flippers

Whales that have teeth snap
up their prey.

Baleen whales gulp water to catch krill.

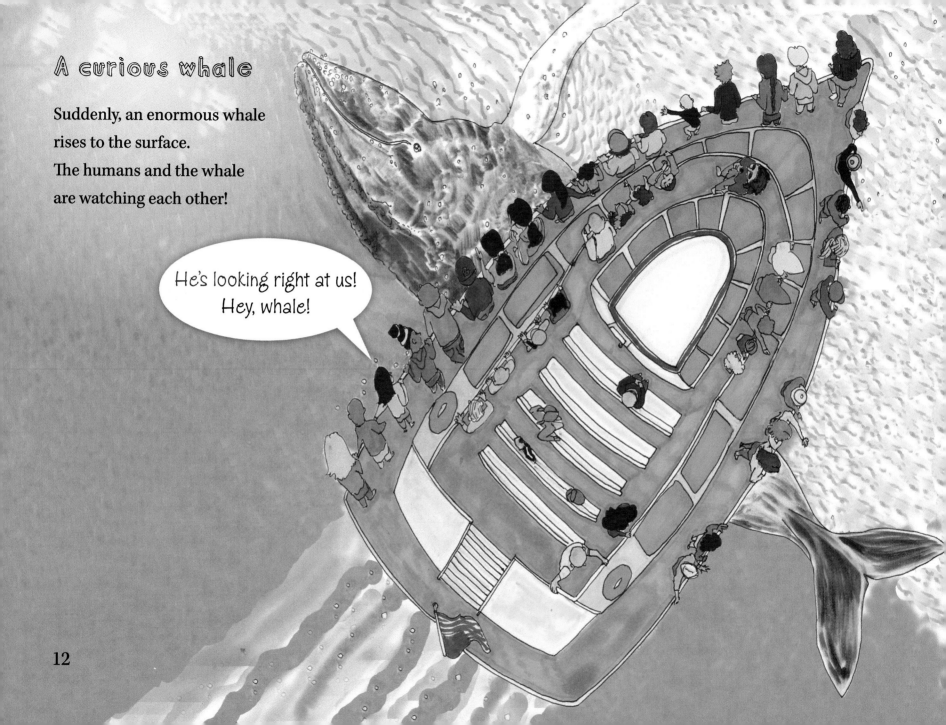

A curious whale

Suddenly, an enormous whale
rises to the surface.
The humans and the whale
are watching each other!

12

This is a young male humpback whale called Hazard. He's curious about our boat.

How can Joanne tell it's Hazard? Humpbacks' tail **flukes** are all different and can be used to identify whales.

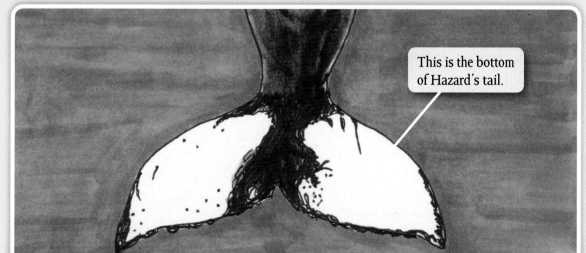

This is the bottom of Hazard's tail.

Joanne also knows Hazard by his scars, which he got from being tangled in some ropes.

13

Humpback surprise

Sometimes humpbacks rocket up out of the ocean and do belly-flops
and slap their tails on the water. Are they sending messages to each other?
Scientists are trying to find out.

WHALE WATC

A whale needs help

Finbacks are the second largest whales in the world, after blue whales. They usually stay deep in the ocean. This one is at the surface because it has a problem. Joanne calls Stormy Mayo, a scientist who can help.

Hi, Stormy. We've spotted a finback whale tangled up in fishing line.

A small boat heads towards the entangled whale. Help is on its way!

People and whales

Most people have stopped hunting whales for food. Many people now try to make the ocean a safer place for whales to live.

It's a wonderful moment when the whale swims free at last.

Hooray!

It's time for the whale watchers to head home. But it isn't over yet ...

Look! There's a **pod** of pilot whales ahead!

Strange creatures

Pilot whales follow the leader,
tagging behind one whale.
Now the whale watch
boat follows them towards
the harbour. The whales only
turn back when the water
gets shallow.

Sometimes whales
that come this close
to shore are lost or sick,
so Joanne reports them.

Joanne's always thinking about the whales, wondering what they're doing.
Tomorrow she'll be back for another whale watch.

Time to go home and walk my dogs! Goodbye, whales and whale watchers!

Glossary

baleen part of the mouth in some types of whale which filters tiny pieces of food from the water

blow a spray of water squirted up when a whale blows air out of its blowhole

blowhole a hole on the head of whales which they breathe through

breed have babies

calf a baby whale

filters separates solid things from water by trapping the bits and letting the water flow away

flukes the pointed parts at the end of whales' tails

pod a group of whales

pollution spoiling the environment by leaving rubbish

21

Whale-watching diary

10.00 a.m.

We set off on Captain Mark's boat and sailed 30 miles to Stellwagen Bank.

11.30 a.m.

We saw a young male humpback whale, Hazard. He did a belly flop right next to the boat!

1.30 p.m.

We saw a finback whale tangled up in ropes. Joanne reported it to Stormy Mayo.

1.45 p.m.

Stormy Mayo got the ropes off the whale.

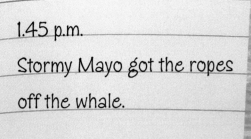

3.30 p.m.

Joanne spotted a pod of pilot whales, following the leader. We followed them back to the harbour. Joanne reported them in case they were lost or sick.

23

🐾 Ideas for reading 🐾

Written by Gillian Howell
Primary Literacy Consultant

Reading objectives:
- predict what might happen on the basis of what has been read so far
- be introduced to non-fiction books that are structured in different ways
- discuss the sequence of events in books and how items of information are related
- read further common exception words, noting unusual correspondences between spelling and sound
- answer and ask questions
- listen to, discuss and express views about a wide range non-fiction

Spoken language objectives:
- use spoken language to develop understanding through speculating, hypothesising, imagining and exploring ideas
- articulate and justify answers, arguments and opinions
- give well-structured descriptions, explanations and narratives for different purposes, including for expressing feelings
- use relevant strategies to build their vocabulary

Curriculum links: Geography, Science

Interest words: ocean, pollution, calf, calves, folks, dolphin, porpoise, minke, material, prey, whom, tangled

Resources: pens, paper, modelling materials, the internet

Word count: 778

Build a context for reading
- Read the title together and discuss the cover illustration. Ask the children to predict what this book will be about. Explain that this book is about real events but written in the style of a graphic novel.

- Turn to the contents page and read the headings with the children. Ask the children if they think the sections should be read in sequence and why.
- Point out the speech bubble on the page and explain that the children should remember to read them as they are an important part of the text.

Understand and apply reading strategies
- Ask the children to read the book quietly and ask them to identify what the aspects of a whale watch are.
- Listen in as they read and prompt as necessary if children struggle with vocabulary, e.g. point out the silent *l* in *calf* on p4 and *calves* on p6.
- As they read, encourage the children to read the illustrations for information on each page, e.g. on p2, ask them how the map relates to the globe. Check that they read all the labels for the illustrations of whales on pp8–9. As they read the names of each whale in the main text, ask them to find it in the illustration.

Develop reading and language comprehension
- Ask children to turn to pp22-23 and read through the diary entries for the whale watch. Discuss each stage and ask children which part of the tour they would have enjoyed the most and why.
- Ask the children to describe the different aspects of a whale watch they discovered by reading the book. Was there anything unexpected or surprising about what happens on a whale watch?